Talking Talia Tattler Tells!

Written by Cheri Alphonse Hayes

Illustrated by Emilio Luis Báez-Rivera

Dedicated to all children... big and small.
Especially, Talia!

Sky's the limit Jordan and Jaden; you are
the wind beneath my wings. I love you two!

Special thanks to Candace Anthony!

Talia loves to talk! She talks from the moment she jumps out of bed, till she falls asleep at night.

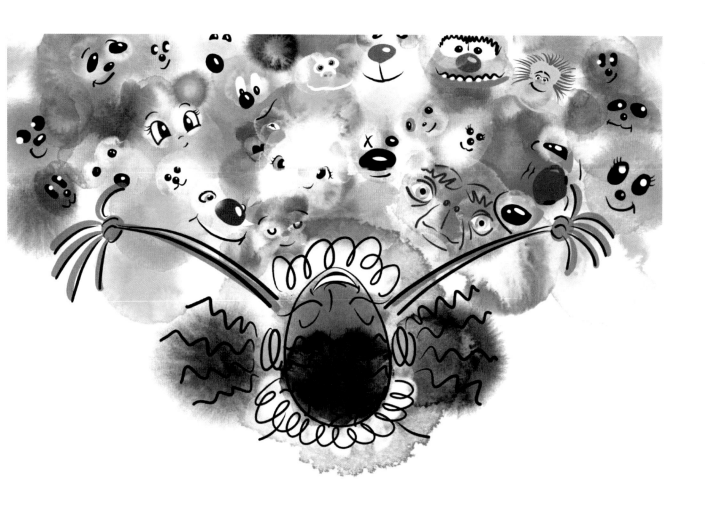

"Good morning toys, dolls, and nothing of

boys!" she exclaims to the room full of colorful

playthings.

Sky's the limit!" she shouts to the birds

perched on the tree outside her window. The

toys and birds are Talia's best friends.

Her brothers, Zach and Tony, are mean.

Every time she opens her mouth to talk to

them, they tell her to put a bubble in it, but

never tell her when to take it out.

They know this is the only way to keep

Talia from talking because she tells their mom

everything!

"Mom," Talia shouts at the top of her lungs,

"Zach and Tony are playing hide-and-seek!"

"There's no harm in playing hide-and-seek,

Talia," Mom replies. "Tattle-tale," they retort in

unison!

"Mom, the boys are riding their bikes

without helmets," Talia bellows frantically!

"Oh my word, that's a no-no boys," Mom shouts

as she runs out after them.

"Mom, Zach's taking the stairs instead of the elevator!" Mom responds in a proud voice, "Now, that is a smart choice, Zach!" Tony looks at Talia and sticks his tongue out at her and whispers, "Tattle-tale!"

Talia did not care; not one bit.

Talia is no different at school. The kids call

her **Talking Talia!** In one whole breath, she

could tell her teacher if her friends used too

much paint in art, swung too high on the swing,

shared snacks at lunch, ran really fast in P.E., or

went to the nurse if they were not sick.

Most days, when Talia goes home from

school, she's sad. She doesn't like being called

Talking Talia.

Mom and Talia's teacher sat down to share

a better way that Talia could work through

understanding tattling and telling. They gave

Talia a big empty lemonade jar, some paper,

and a pencil.

Reporting the Facts

Name: _____

Incident:_____

_____

_____

- ○ Did anyone get hurt?_____
- ○ Can others get hurt doing this?_____
- ○ Does an adult need to help solve the problem?_____

If you checked yes to these questions, this is a good story to report.

"A good reporter always gets the facts before reporting," her teacher told her. "Before you report any news, fill out this information form with all the facts," mom added. When you have filled your jar with stories, you can have the spotlight to share them all.

Talia became excited and felt more

important than ever! She set out to collect her

stories. She knew her jar would be filled soon.

A day went by and Talia's jar was not full.

Two days later, still not full. By the end of the

week, she was so engaged in playing with Zach

and Tony, she left her jar at home.

"Honey, you're forgetting your jar," Mom

yells, as Talia runs out the door. "No need mom.

My friends are solving their own problems and

the grown-ups are fixing the bigger problems.

And... I can't play with my friends if I am

holding a jar" Talia replies with a smile!

The End...

of a new beginning!

In the story, when did Talia...

Tattle	Tell

Let's Talk!

1. Who were the main characters in the story?
2. How would you describe Talia?
3. Were Zach and Tony mean?
4. Did Talia know the difference between tattling and telling?
5. Why did Talia's mom and teacher decide to help?
6. Talia thought she would collect many stories to share. What do you think happened when Talia set out to collect her stories?
7. Look back at the page where Talia is playing with her brothers. How does this illustration make you feel? Why?
8. Did Talia forget her jar?
9. Does Talia learn the difference between tattling and telling? Explain your answer.
10. What does the author mean when she wrote, the end of a new beginning?

Option 1: Write or draw a short story sharing the events you envision that took place when Talia attempted to collect stories for her jar.

Option 2: Write or draw a short story telling how the events would be different if Talia's mom and teacher did not step in to help.

About The Author

Keeping true to her roots, although leaving her land of birth at the age of 10, Cheri Alphonse Hayes is a patriot and a die-hard lover of the island of St. Lucia. She believes in keeping her cultural origins and ancestral foundation alive through language (creole), dialect, events and travel. As the eldest girl of her parents, it has always been in her nature to nurture and care for children through mentoring and teaching. Now, a mother of two young men, Jordan and Jaden, Cheri creates opportunities for her children to learn and engage in their rich heritage in the United States as well as the Caribbean.

Currently, Cheri is married to Carleton J. Hayes of Newark, NJ and resides in Japan where she is employed by the Department of Defense Education Activity. Follow her on Facebook at https://www.facebook.com/CheriAlphonseHayes/

About The Illustrator

Coming from a loving family in Puerto Rico, Emilio Luis Báez-Rivera has always enjoyed being surrounded by academics and the arts. He began sketching his own drawings early on and was introduced to music by his father. Emilio Luis earned his BFA from the University of Puerto Rico and his MA TESOL from the Inter American University. He has worked as a freelance artist, graphic artist, and a Visual Arts Teacher. He was awarded the high honor of the Teacher of the Year Award in 2013. Currently, he is an ESL teacher for the Department of Defense Education Activity in Japan. Emilio Luis loves sharing his passion for education and the arts in the classroom with students of all ages. He plays several instruments, especially enjoys visual arts, and loves to learn new things daily.

Emilio Luis is married to Ms. Mayra Peña, and is a proud father of his two sons; Elijah Immanu'El and Tristan Isaiah.

Talia

Made in the USA
Monee, IL
04 August 2020